WAY OF THE NINJA

ADAPTED BY TRACEY WEST

SCHOLASTIC INC.
NEW YORK   TORONTO   LONDON   AUCKLAND
SYDNEY   MEXICO CITY   NEW DELHI   HONG KONG

ISBN 978-0-545-40113-5

12 11 10 9 8 7 6 5   12 13 14 15 16/0

Printed in the U.S.A.   40
First printing, November 2011

MEET KAI

Clang! Clang! Clang!

Kai pounded metal into the shape of a sword. He dipped the hot metal into a bucket of cold water. Then he pulled out . . . a crooked sword.

"You made it too quickly, Kai," said his sister, Nya. "Be patient."

"Don't worry, Nya," Kai said. "I'm going to be a better blacksmith than Dad ever was!"

An old man with a white beard walked into the shop.

"These are tools for a samurai," he said, looking around. "But nothing for a ninja."

"Ninja?" Kai laughed. "There are no ninja in these parts, old man." Kai turned to Nya. When he looked back, the old man was gone.

That night, an army of skeleton warriors roared into Kai's village on their Skull Motorbikes. Their king, Samukai, led them in his Skull Truck.

"Let me go first!" whined Nuckal, a skeleton commander. "I'm dying to go down there!"

"Nitwit! You're already dead!" barked his partner, Kruncha.

"Besides, Master Samukai, you said *I* could go first," Kruncha added.

"Sorry, boys, this one is mine," Samukai said. "Just find that map!"

Samukai's red eyes gleamed like fire. "Attack!" he yelled.

ENTER THE SKELETONS

Vroom! Vroom! Vroom!
The warriors zoomed into the village on their Skull Motorbikes. Samukai steered the Skull Truck toward Kai's blacksmith shop. The villagers screamed and ran away.

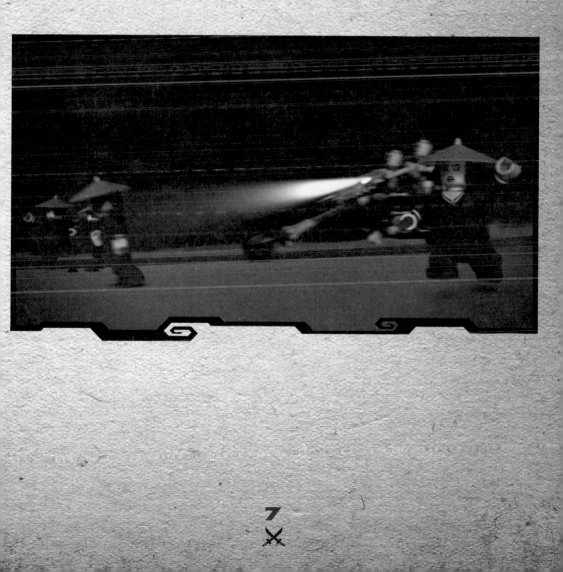

Kai raced out to fight the warriors. He swung his samurai sword, and one of the skeletons' heads popped off.

"Ow!" Kai cried, as the skeleton bit his ankle. "Bite this!"

He kicked the skeleton head like a football. The other warriors clapped as the skull flew through the air.

Nya stepped up and whacked two of the warriors with her staff.

"You should have stayed back," Kai told her.

"And let *you* have all the fun?" Nya asked.

While Kai and Nya fought the skeletons, Nuckal and Kruncha snuck into the blacksmith shop.

Inside Kai's shop, Nuckal put on a samurai hat. "You're not looking hard enough!" Kruncha said, bopping him on the head.

"Owww! No, *you're* not looking hard enough!" cried Nuckal, throwing the helmet at Kruncha.

Bam! Pow! Crunch! The two skeletons slapped at each other. Kruncha banged into the wall. The sign over the door fell down.

The two skeletons gasped when they saw something hidden behind the sign. "The map!" they shouted.

KAI'S MISSION

Outside, Samukai leaped down from his truck. He grabbed four knives and attacked Kai.

As Kai fell back, a cry rang out. *"Ninjago!"*

A spinning gold tornado whirled between Kai and Samukai. The tornado smacked into Samukai. When it stopped spinning, the old man from the shop stood there.

"Sensei Wu!" cried Samukai. "Your Spinjitzu looks rusty."

With a grin, Samukai threw his knives. They slammed into an old water tower. The tower started to fall.

"Ninjago!" With a yell, Sensei Wu spun and picked up Kai before the tower could land on him.

Laughing, Samukai jumped into his truck. "Garmadon says to get the girl," he growled. Kruncha pulled a lever. A skeleton claw swung out of the truck and grabbed Nya! Then the Skull Truck sped away.

"Nya!" screamed Kai. He picked up his sword. "I'm going to get my sister back."

"Where they go, no mortal may follow," Sensei Wu told him. "That was Samukai, King of the Underworld. If he's working for Lord Garmadon, things are worse than I thought."

A TALE OF TWO BROTHERS

"Why did they come here? What do they want?" Kai asked.

"Long before time had a name, Ninjago was created by the first Spinjitzu Master," Sensei Wu began. "He used the Four Weapons of Spinjitzu: the Scythe of Quakes, the Nunchuks of Lightning, the Shurikens of Ice, and the Sword of Fire."

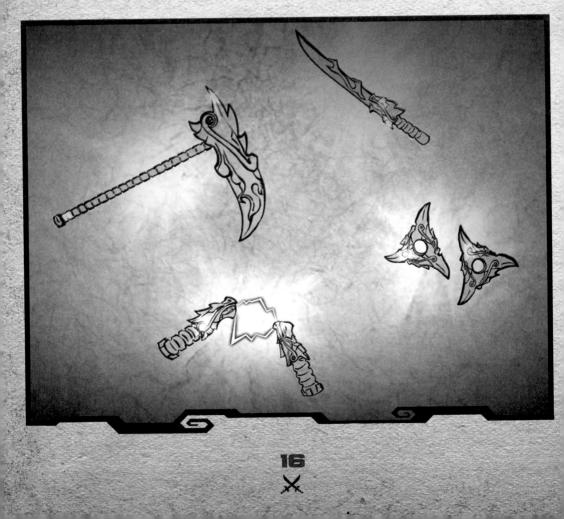

"When the master passed away, his two sons swore to protect them," Sensei Wu went on. "But the oldest was taken over by darkness. He wanted the Weapons for his own. A battle between brothers broke out. The oldest was struck down and sent to the Underworld."

"The younger brother hid the Weapons in four different places," said Sensei Wu. "He sent a Guardian to protect each one. And then he gave the map to an honest man to hide. That honest man was your father."

Kai's eyes grew wide.

"The older brother is Lord Garmadon,"
Sensei Wu told Kai. "I must find those
Weapons before he does!"

"You're the younger brother?" Kai asked.
"Then you came here looking for the map?"

Sensei Wu shook his head. "No," he said.
"I came for something greater. You!"

"You have the fire inside, Kai," Sensei Wu said. "You can help me."

Kai turned away. "I don't care about all that. I just need to get my sister."

Sensei Wu twirled around and knocked down Kai with his staff. He put his foot on Kai's chest.

"If you want to get your sister back, you must learn to tame the fire inside," said Sensei Wu. "Only if you master Spinjitzu will you be ready to face Lord Garmadon."

Kai knew Sensei Wu was right. Together they began the long journey to Sensei Wu's dojo.

NINJA-IN-TRAINING

"Complete this training course before I finish my tea," Sensei Wu told Kai. "Then, we will see if you are ready."

Day after day, Kai tried to complete the course. He battled wood soldiers on a spinning platform. But he smacked into one of the soldiers and fell off.

"Fail," Sensei Wu said.

Kai tried to jump across a row of spinning spikes. Once again, he fell.

"Fail," said Sensei Wu.

Kai failed and failed and failed again. But he didn't give up. He kept training.

Finally, Kai got it right. He dodged weapons. He jumped on pillars. He fought wooden soldiers with his sword. And he did it all before the sensei finished his tea.

"So now can I learn Spinjitzu?" Kai asked.

"You already have," Sensei Wu replied. "Your final test comes tomorrow."

AND THEN THERE WERE FOUR

That night, Kai practiced Spinjitzu while he brushed his teeth.

"Take that! And that! And this!" he cried, spinning around.

Then he stopped. He was surrounded by three ninja dressed in black!

Kai threw his toothbrush at the ninja.
Then he leaped onto a ceiling beam.
One of the ninja jumped in front of him.
   "Hi-yah!" Kai cried, knocking him down.
But another ninja tossed him outside.
Kai landed in the training yard. He made
the platforms and pillars spin.

The spinning platforms slammed into the ninja, but they jumped back to their feet.

Bam! Pow! Kick! All three ninja attacked Kai. He fought back bravely.

Sensei Wu's voice rang out. "Stop!"

The three ninja bowed. "Yes, Sensei."

"They're your students, too?" Kai asked, and the sensei nodded. "This was my final test, wasn't it?"

"What is the meaning of this, Master?" one ninja asked.

"Each of you is in tune with a different element," Sensei Wu explained. "But first — *Ninjago!*"

Sensei Wu began to spin. He whirled around the ninja. When he stopped, the ninja were all wearing different uniforms!

Kai wore a red uniform. "Kai, Master of Fire," Sensei Wu said. Then he pointed to a ninja in a blue uniform. "Jay is blue, Master of Lightning."

"Black ninja is Cole," Sensei Wu went on. "Solid as rock. Master of Earth." Finally, he approached the ninja in white. "And white ninja is Zane, Master of Ice."

"You four are the chosen ones who will protect the Weapons of Spinjitzu from Lord Garmadon!" Sensei Wu told them.

"But what about my sister?" demanded Kai.

Jay gasped. "We're saving a girl? Is she cute? Does she like blue?"

"When we find the Weapons, we will find your sister, Kai," Sensei Wu promised. "It is time! We must go to the first Weapon."

Cole stepped up. "Hold on a minute. You said you were going to teach us Spinjitzu."

"Spinjitzu is inside each of you," Sensei Wu replied. "But it will only be unlocked when the key is ready to be found."

"Great! Now we have to find a key," Jay complained.

"I feel like he's taking us for a ride," Cole added.

Kai pulled on his red hood. "If it means finding my sister, then sign me up!"

The four ninja followed Sensei Wu into the night.